Back to Zero

by Dr. Joy

illustrated by
jeanelle tabaranza

...because some days are not so easy.

Back to Zero
by Dr. Joy
Published by EduMatch®
PO Box 150324, Alexandria, VA 22315

www.edumatchpublishing.com

ISBN-13: 978-1-970133-87-5

I dedicate this book to my husband and children who have brought so much joy to my world. I'd like to thank my dad and mom who gave me the nickname *Joy*. This name has empowered me through life's ups and downs. Lastly, I am so grateful for all of the beautiful students that I have crossed paths with over the last two decades. They have been some of my greatest teachers.

Much love,
Dr. Joy

You will find a joy in overcoming obstacles.
-Helen Keller

There are times in school when
I can't handle the load.

It feels like my brain is going to explode.

I'm reaching a level 10, a very scary space.

0 1 2 3

I need to get back to zero, a much safer place.

I hate that it happens when everyone is around.

In the midst of it all, I'm having a meltdown.

If you feel you're reaching 10 and don't know what to do.

I have a few ideas that will surely get you through.

10

Take nice slow deep breath
Try this for a while.

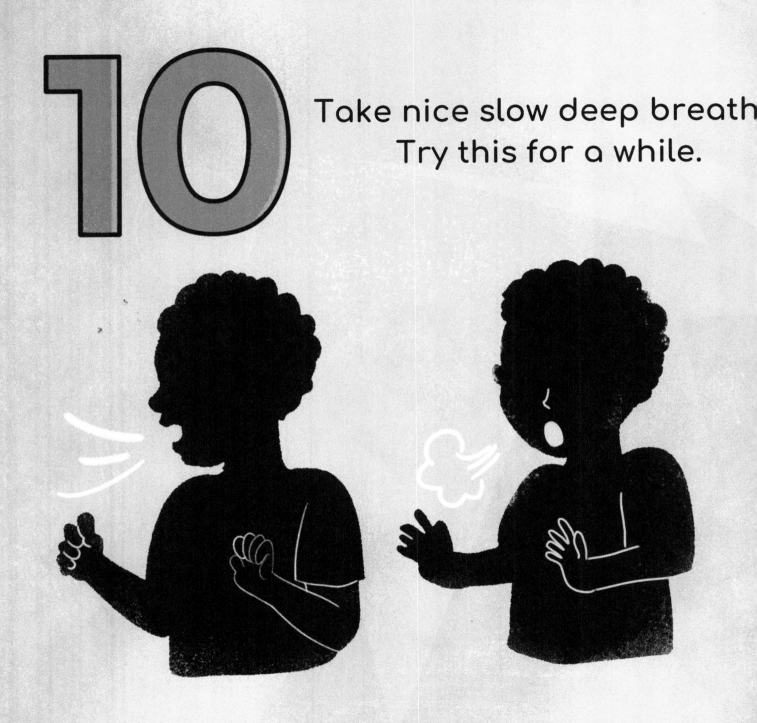

9

Switch that unhappy thought with one that makes you smile.

8

There isn't anything wrong with taking a short rest.

Safe Place

7 Talk with someone special who knows you the best.

6 You might prefer to take a mindful stroll.

5

Keep an object near
that is dear to your soul.

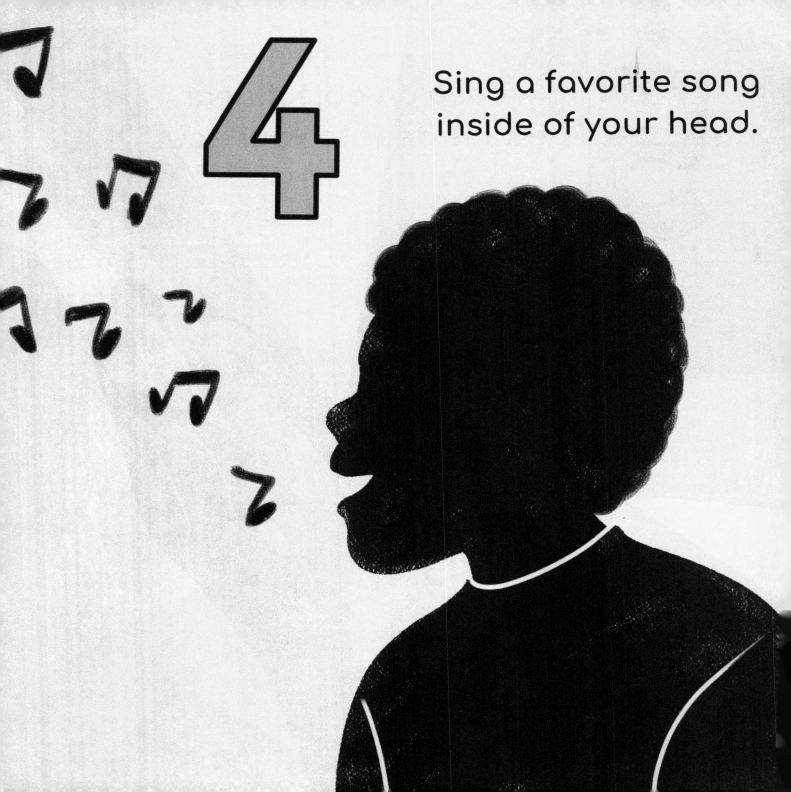

4 Sing a favorite song inside of your head.

3

Imagine being in your happy place instead.

A cool sip of water works very well too.

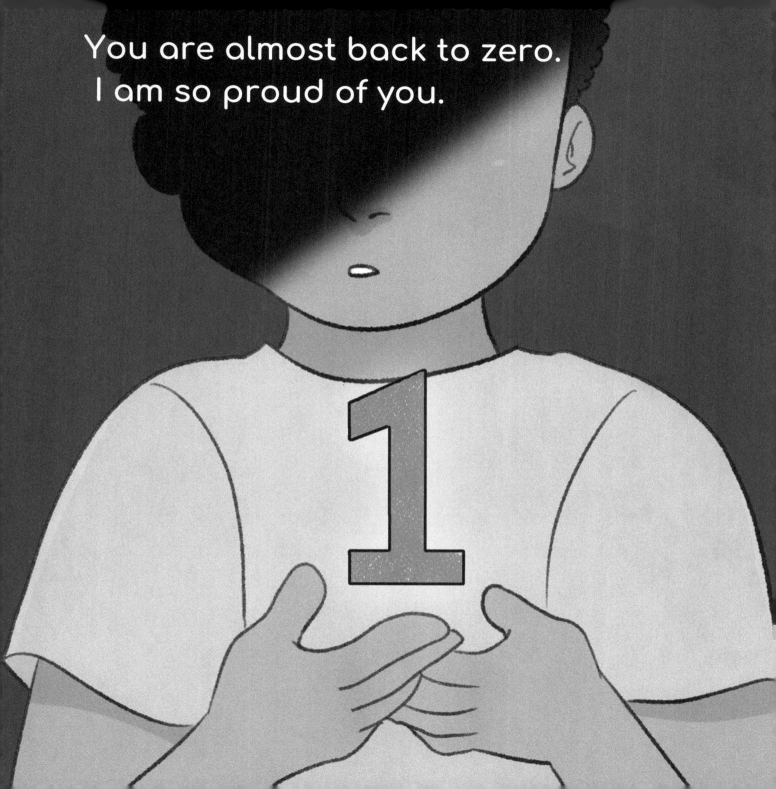

Try one of these ideas before you reach a 10. You can make it back to 0 and feel yourself aga

Discussion Questions

❏ Describe situations in the classroom that make you feel like you are reaching a level 10.

❏ What are some words to describe what it feels like when you are reaching a level 10?

❏ How does your mind and body feel right before you reach a level 10?

❏ What is one way you can get back to zero?

❏ Who can help you get back to zero?

❏ What can you do if you see one of your classmates reaching a level 10?

❏ What can we all do to help fill our classroom with joy?

Follow-up Activities

❏ Create a poster or board dedicated to coping strategies.
❏ Have students create an individual book of coping strategies.
❏ Create a space in the classroom where students can take a mindful break.
❏ Discuss ways students can get the teacher's attention when they feel they are reaching a level 10.
❏ Have ongoing discussions about the classroom community.

About the Author

Hi, I'm Dr. Joy.

I wrote this book because I truly believe that all kids need to feel that school is a joyful place where they can learn and grow. They also need to understand that challenges are a part of learning and growing and that some days are not going to be easy. There are times when **we all** feel like we are reaching a level 10. We can all benefit from learning how to navigate challenges. No one wants to feel that they can't recover from a bad moment or day. My hope is that schools will use this resource to open spaces that support students' social and emotional needs, and embrace challenges with empathy and love.

You can find additional resources for this story on my site
joyworkedu.com.

EduMatch Publishing

CPSIA information can be obtained
at www.ICGtesting.com
Printed in the USA
LVHW060909020920
664819LV00014B/1313